Little Daruma
and the Little Rabbits

A Japanese Children's Tale

Author and Illustrator

Satoshi Kako was born in 1926 at Takefu City in Fukui, Japan. He received his Doctorate in Engineering from Tokyo University and is a Certified Consulting Engineer of Chemistry. Mr Kako joined the campus Drama Circle and participated in volunteer groups from 1949 onwards, organizing and helping in children's groups for 25 years. He was also the editor and publisher of *Picture Story*, the newsletter of the Kami Shibai study group. Mr Kako's first children's book, *People of Dam Construction*, was published in 1959. Other books in this acclaimed series of illustrated scientific books include *River*, *Sea*, *The Earth*, *The Universe* and *The Human Being*.

Mr Kako has written almost 500 children's books on natural science, history, literature and the arts. In 1990, his book *Pyramid: Its History and Science* was awarded the Japanese Scientific Book Prize of the Year. Mr Kako is a visiting lecturer at Tokyo University and Yokohama National University, and is a consultant in the fields of education and science. He lives in Fujisawa City in Kanagawa.

Translator's Note

In Japan, *daruma* are dolls representing the Indian priest Bodhidharma, the founder of Zen Buddhism. They are reputed to make wishes come true, and the custom is for a person to first paint one eye of the *daruma* and place it on the family shrine, then to paint the other eye when the wish is fulfilled. *Daruma* have weighted bottoms so they always roll upright. This shows their spirit of perseverance! *Tangesazen* is the name of a famous warrior with one eye and one arm. *Zatoichi* is the name of a famous blind swordsman. *Tangesazen* and *Zatoichi* are the stars of numerous popular movies.

Translators

Peter Howlett was born and raised in Hokkaido. He is an EFL teacher at Hakodate La Salle Junior & Senior High Schools. He is also the chairperson of the Southern Hokkaido Natural Energy Initiative, a group that promotes the use of alternative energy.

Richard McNamara is the director of the Aso Wildcats environmental group (AsoWildcats@ hotmail.com) and specializes in the poetry of Edmund Spenser and the psychology of stress and clinical biofeedback.

Peter and Richard are officials of the Dr Wildcat Committee, a group dedicated to publicizing environmental issues through the works of Miyazawa Kenji, Vandana Shiva, David Suzuki and Oiwa Keibo, among others. They are also regular contributors to the *Shukan Kinyobi* magazine.

Published by Tuttle Publishing, an imprint of Periplus Editions (HK) Ltd.

Text & Illustrations © Satoshi Kako, 1972
First published in 1972 by Fukuinkan Shoten Publishers, Inc., Tokyo, Japan
First Tuttle edition, 2002
All rights reserved

LCC Card No. 2002108055
ISBN 0-8048-3349-4
ISBN 4-8053-0686-6 (for sale in Japan)

Distributed by:

Japan
Tuttle Publishing
Yaekari Building, 3F
5-4-12 Osaki, Shinagawa-ku
Tokyo 141-0032
Tel: (03) 5437 0171, Fax: (03) 5437 0755
Email: tuttle-sales@gol.com

North America
Tuttle Publishing
Airport Industrial Park
364 Innovation Drive
North Clarendon, VT 05759-9436
Tel: (802) 773 8930, Fax: (802) 773 6993
Email: info@tuttlepublishing.com

Asia Pacific
Berkeley Books Pte. Ltd.
130 Joo Seng Road #06-01/03
Singapore 368357
Tel: (65) 6280 1330, Fax: (65) 6280 6290
Email: inquiries@periplus.com.sg

08 07 06 05 04 03 8 7 6 5 4 3 2

Printed in Singapore

Little Daruma and the Little Rabbits

A Japanese Children's Tale

by Satoshi Kako

translated by Peter Howlett

and Richard McNamara

TUTTLE PUBLISHING

Boston • Rutland, Vermont • Tokyo

It's the day after a heavy snowfall and everything is blanketed in white.

Little Daruma and his sister, Little Darumako, are playing in the snow.

4

They decide to make a snowman.

"Now what shall we use for the eyes?"

wonders Little Darumako.

Little Daruma has a great idea . . .

"Apples!" he says. And just as he says this, Mother Daruma comes out and gives him and Little Darumako two shiny red apples.

Little Daruma puts an apple into the eye of the snowman. But the apple falls out, hits him on the head and . . .

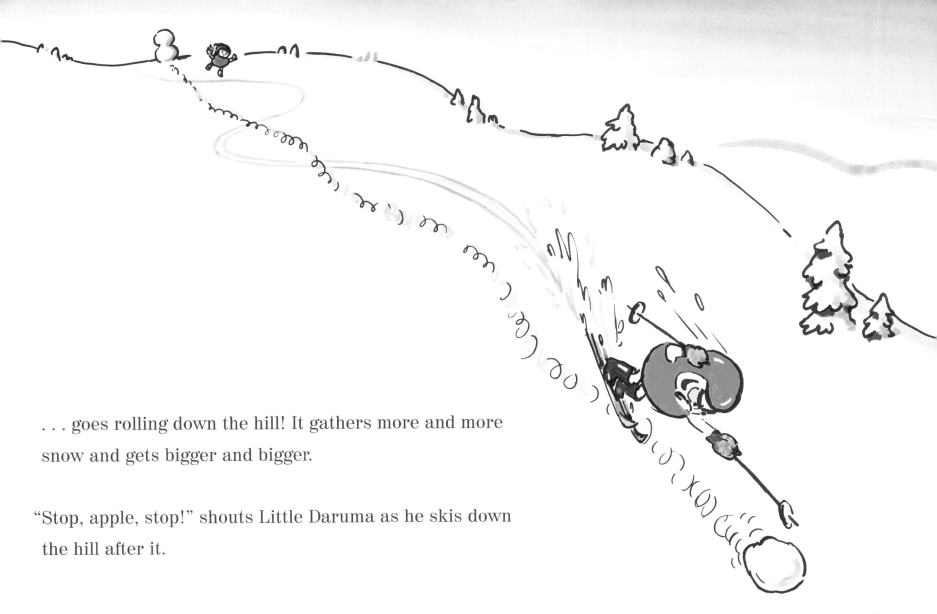

. . . goes rolling down the hill! It gathers more and more snow and gets bigger and bigger.

"Stop, apple, stop!" shouts Little Daruma as he skis down the hill after it.

Two rabbits named Roy and Ruby are playing
at the bottom of the hill.

The apple hits Roy Rabbit with a loud "BOOM!"
and flies into Ruby Rabbit's arms.

Little Daruma says, "Thank you both! Without this apple,
my snowman would have become a Tangesazen snowman!"

Roy Rabbit says, "A Tange-what snowman? What is that?"
Little Daruma says, "Tangesazen is the name of a strong
and famous swordsman who only has one eye and one arm!"

Ruby Rabbit asks, "What's a snowman?"
Little Daruma replies, "A snowman is a
man made up of two balls of snow, with
apples and sticks for its eyes, nose, mouth
and arms!"

Ruby Rabbit asks again, "But why is a snowman
without an apple a Tangesazen snowman?"

Little Daruma scratches his head and says,
"Come with me, I'll just show you the answer!"

The two rabbits are delighted and they hippity-hop up the hill to Little Daruma's house.

Little Daruma skis up the hill after them, out of breath and going hippity-huff, hippity-huff.

"This is a snowman," says Little Daruma.

Snowman

Tangesazen Snowman

"And this is a Tangesazen snowman!"

"Now I understand!" says Ruby Rabbit. Then Little Daruma uses his skis to make ears for his snowman. The two rabbits are delighted and hop about saying, "This must be a snowrabbit!"

Snowrabbit

13

Next, Little Darumako puts some snow on a plate. Using leaves and berries, she makes a baby snowrabbit.

Baby Snowrabbit

Little Daruma also puts some snow on a tray. Using pine cones, pine needles and bamboo leaves, he makes a grandfather snowrabbit.

Roy and Ruby Rabbit are delighted at all the different snowrabbits. Then, from behind the snowman comes . . .

Grandfather Snowrabbit

. . . a rabbit puppet!

"Hello, little rabbits!" says the puppet, "How are you today?"

Hopping up and down, the rabbits ask, "Can you show us how to make a rabbit puppet?"

1. Push in three fingers of a left-hand glove.

2. Fold-up the wrist-band of the glove.

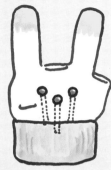

3. Stick in three matchsticks for the eyes and nose.

How to Make a Rabbit Puppet

"Of course," says Little Darumako, "It's easy!"

5. Put your right hand into the glove.

6. Place the rabbit head glove on top of this glove.

4. Push in the thumb of a right-hand glove.

Just then, Mother Daruma calls out, "It's tea-time!"
"Hello, Mrs Daruma," say the two rabbits, bowing.
"My, what good manners you have," says Mother
Daruma. "Won't you join us for tea?"

"Thank you!" say the rabbits, and everyone runs
  into the warm house.

Mother Daruma has made all sorts of wonderful dishes.
As she pours everyone a hot cup of tea, Little
Darumako shows the little rabbits how to
fold a paper napkin into a rabbit.

Roy and Ruby Rabbit are having the time of their lives, drinking tea and making napkin rabbits.

How to Make a Napkin Rabbit

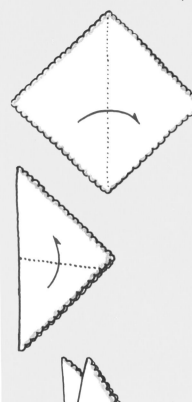

1. Fold a napkin in half to make a triangle.

2. Fold one end up to make two ears.

3. Fold over the bottom right corner to form the face.

4. Use a pencil to draw in the eyes.

How to Make an Apple Rabbit

1. Cut an apple in half, and then cut each half into thirds. Be careful when using the knife.

2. Peel the skin as shown to form two ears.

3. Peel just one side of the apple.

4. Use apple seeds to form the eyes.

"Here are some apples for you," says Mother Daruma as she shows them how to make rabbits and *darumas* with apples.

"That's wonderful!" say the rabbits as they bite into the crisp apples.

How to Make an Apple *Daruma*

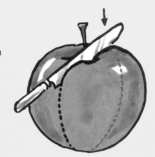

1. Cut an apple in half. Be careful when using the knife.

2. Cut into the apple to just about halfway.

3. Cut down to the first cutting and remove this piece.

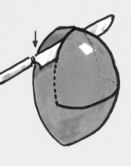

4. Use apple seeds and a small slice of apple for the eyes and mouth.

After tea, Little Daruma makes something else for his new friends. By arranging a teacup, a plate, two spoons, two knives and two forks around on the table, Little Daruma makes a tea set rabbit.

How to Make a Tea Set Rabbit

1. Line up two spoons to make the ears.

2. Set a teacup upside-down on top of the spoons.

"You're good at making all sorts of rabbits!" says Roy Rabbit. "This is so much fun, I wish we could stay here all day!" says Ruby Rabbit.

3. Turn a plate over to make the body.

4. Line up two forks and two knives to make the arms and legs.

"But it's getting late, Ruby," says Roy Rabbit, "and we
   should be going home."
"I guess you're right," says Ruby Rabbit. "Thank you
   all so much for tea!"

"What good manners you have!" says Mother Daruma.
"Little Daruma, why don't you make your friends some
   rabbit hats before they go?"

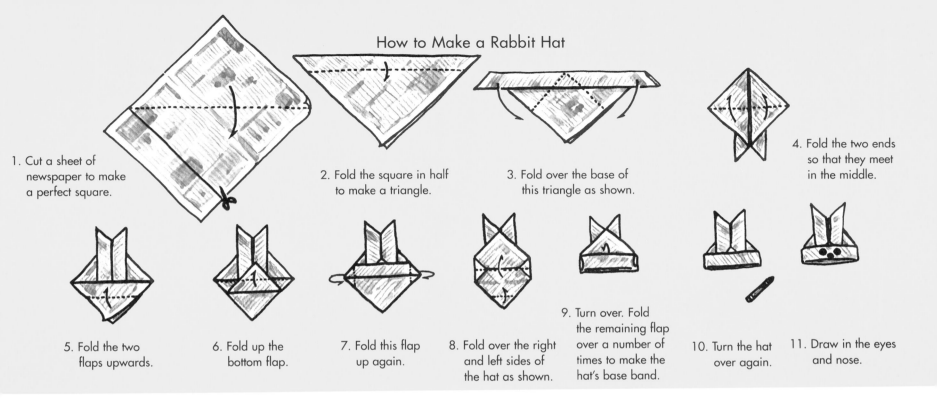

How to Make a Rabbit Hat

1. Cut a sheet of newspaper to make a perfect square.

2. Fold the square in half to make a triangle.

3. Fold over the base of this triangle as shown.

4. Fold the two ends so that they meet in the middle.

5. Fold the two flaps upwards.

6. Fold up the bottom flap.

7. Fold this flap up again.

8. Fold over the right and left sides of the hat as shown.

9. Turn over. Fold the remaining flap over a number of times to make the hat's base band.

10. Turn the hat over again.

11. Draw in the eyes and nose.

"Thank you both for the wonderful hats!" say Roy and Ruby Rabbit together.

When they go outside, everyone is surprised to find that the apples on the snowman are gone.

Little Daruma says, "This must be a Zatoichi snowman!"

"A Zatoichi snowman?" asks Roy Rabbit. "What's that?"

"Zatoichi is the name of a famous blind swordsman," explains Little Daruma.

"But why is a snowman without eyes a Zatoichi snowman?" asks Ruby Rabbit.

"Well, let me see . . ." says Little Daruma, scratching his head. "I'll save that for next time!"

"Goodbye, Little Daruma and Little Darumako!" says Roy Rabbit.

"Goodbye, Zatoichi snowman!" says Ruby Rabbit.

"Goodbye, little rabbits. Come again soon!" say the two Darumas to their new friends.

And off go the rabbits with their new hats, hippity-hopping their way home.

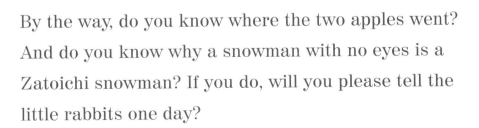

By the way, do you know where the two apples went? And do you know why a snowman with no eyes is a Zatoichi snowman? If you do, will you please tell the little rabbits one day?

日本を代表する絵本作家、かこさとしが作り出す心温まるファンタジーの世界。1967年に発行されて以来300万部の売上げを誇るだるまちゃんシリーズは、今も変わらず多くの人々に愛されつづけています。だるまちゃんのゆかいな冒険を通して映し出されるのは、子供の視線で世界を見つめている作者の想像力にほかなりません。だるまちゃんと仲良し家族が住む世界では、民話に登場するクラシックなキャラクターたちが現代に暮らしているのです！そして、そのほんわかしたイメージ画と楽しい語り口に触れれば、子供たちが繰り返しページをめくる訳も理解できるでしょう。初めて英訳されたこのだるまちゃんシリーズは、さらなる読者を魅了することと思います。

雪がつもったある日、だるまちゃんとだるまこちゃんは、2ひきのうさぎちゃんとお友だちになります。雪うさぎや、手ぶくろ人形を作ったり、だるまちゃんは楽しいあそびをいろいろおしえてくれます。いつもゆかいなことがいっぱいの「だるまちゃん」シリーズ英語版第3作です。

文・絵：かこさとし（加古里子） 1926年福井県武生市生まれ。東京大学工学部応用化学科卒。大学卒業後、昭和電工研究所に勤めながら、子供会を中心とする活動から絵本を制作するようになる。絵本作家として40数年間に作品数は約500点に及び、その分野は「自然科学」、「社会」、「歴史」、「文学」、「芸術」と多岐にわたっている。現在5作品になる大人気の「だるまちゃん」シリーズをはじめ、「だむのおじさんたち」、「とこちゃんはどこ」、「どろぼうがっこう」、「からすのパンやさん」などのお話絵本のほか、「かわ」、「海」、「地球」、「宇宙」、「人間」など大型科学絵本を刊行。1990年に刊行された「ピラミッド—その歴史と科学」は、日本科学読み物賞を受賞した。 工学博士。神奈川県藤沢市在住。

訳：ピーター・ハウレット 北海道生まれ。函館ラ・サール中・高等学校で教鞭を執る。
リチャード・マクナマラ イギリス生まれ。阿蘇ワイルドキャッツの代表として活動するかたわら、阿蘇ワイルドキャッツラジオ局を運営。阿蘇在住、大学講師。
二人は環境団体「山猫博士の会」のメンバー。宮沢賢治やヴァンダナ・シヴァ等の作品を通じて、環境問題に取り組んでいる。絵本「ぐりとぐら」シリーズのほか "Sushi for Kids"、"The Ainu"（タトル出版刊）の翻訳も担当。

welcome to the world of
Little Daruma

Tuttle for Kids books presents Asia's finest and most popular children's stories, like the *Little Daruma* series. These immensely popular books have won numerous awards and are among the best-loved children's books in Japan. With their sparkling illustrations and enchanting stories, these classic books are sure to delight.

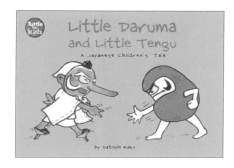

ISBN: 0-8048-3347-8 (World)
ISBN: 4-8053-0684-X (Japan only)

ISBN: 0-8048-3348-6 (World)
ISBN: 4-8053-0685-8 (Japan only)

ISBN: 0-8048-3349-4 (World)
ISBN: 4-8053-0686-6 (Japan only)